ANGEL IN CHARGE

ANGEL IN CHARGE

Judy Delton

Illustrated by Leslie Morrill

A Yearling Book

Published by
Dell Publishing
a division of
Bantam Doubleday Dell Publishing Group, Inc.
666 Fifth Avenue
New York, New York 10103

ISBN: 0-440-40264-6

Reprinted by arrangement with Houghton Mifflin Company

Printed in the United States of America

February 1990

10 9 8 7 6 5 4 3 2 1

CWO

*For Dorothy Ofstead Tucker with love and
renewal, and memories of our
Angel-Rags years in Oakdale.*

CONTENTS

1

MRS. O'LEARY'S NEWS

Angel O'Leary sat on her back steps smiling. Not long ago she had sat there almost every day, frowning. Her mother's friend Alyce always used to ask, "Doesn't that child ever smile?" when she came to visit. And her mother would answer, "No, she always looks like she just lost her best friend."

But now Angel had a best friend. Her name was Edna. After what seemed like years to Angel, her mother allowed her to cross streets and go off her own block and even to stay overnight at Edna's house occasionally — just when Angel had begun to think she would be home forever, taking care of Rags, her four-year-old brother. Rags would soon start kindergarten, and Angel looked forward to that day. Even though she enjoyed a great deal of new freedom, she still saw Rags more than she saw anyone else.

Rags's real name was Theodore, and Angel's real name was Caroline. They lived in an old green house in a small Wisconsin town. Angel went to St. Mary's School.

Angel began to hum a tune as she sat on the steps. This sunny Saturday stretched before her unplanned and challenging.

She thought of what she might do with her day. She could call Edna, and they could ride their bikes down to the swimming pool to watch the men raking the dead leaves out of it. Or they could go to the playground and climb on the jungle gym.

Or she and Edna could go to the department store downtown and look at the new fall clothes that were coming in and the new ponytail holders and barrettes and even the shiny rows of perfume bottles and tubes of lipstick.

Or they could just sit on Angel's front porch swing and eat cookies and read books. They each took five books out of the library every week. Mrs. Dolan, the librarian, told their mothers that they were her most loyal patrons.

Rags was digging under the porch. He wasn't visible because of the latticework, but Angel knew he was making a city with streets and roads and fields and houses and swimming pools that were filled with real water. This city was going to have a Grand Canyon in it, and Rags was busy every day digging it good and deep. When Mrs. O'Leary learned what he was up to, she said not to dig too deep because the house might fall over. But Rags didn't know how deep "too deep" was, and his mother had no way of knowing either, because she couldn't see it since the space under the porch was only big enough for Rags or Angel to climb into.

"Angel?" Rags called now, in a voice that sounded far away and hollow. "Are you going to play with me today?"

"I don't know," said Angel, savoring the day ahead. "I might go somewhere with Edna." She knew the next thing Rags would say. She bet herself a nickel he would say, "Can I come, too?" But only silence came from under the porch.

With her mind on the day's plans, Angel had almost forgotten about the nickel bet to herself when the latticework swung outward and Rags's muddy face appeared.

"Can I come, too?"

Angel had won a nickel from herself. "Maybe," she started to reply. Then she remembered how it irritated her when her mother said that. "Probably not," she answered instead.

In the house, Angel heard the telephone ring. She heard the sound of her mother's shoes tip-tapping across the tile floor as she went to answer it.

"Well!" said Mrs. O'Leary on the phone. "Oh, I don't think so, Beth . . . Yes, but . . . Really? . . . Yes, it would be nice, but . . . I don't . . . Yes, I'll surely think about it, Beth."

Angel's mother hung up the phone and came to the back door. She wore a worried expression on her face most of the time, one that made her look older than she really was.

"Do you think it looks like rain, Angel?" she said, looking more troubled than usual.

Angel shook her head. The sky looked clear to her.

"You'll never guess who was on the phone just now, dear."

Angel didn't feel like guessing. Her mother met lots of people at work. It could be anyone.

"It was your Aunt Beth!"

Although she didn't see her very often, Angel was very fond of her Aunt Beth.

"Is she coming to visit?" asked Angel.

"Not exactly," said her mother. "She wants me to take a trip with her. Imagine my going on a trip!"

"Where to?" said Angel, more interested now.

"To Canada. She has business there, and the hotel room would be all paid for. She's leaving in a week. She wants me to go along, and after she takes care of the business, she says we would have a vacation — rent a car and drive around Canada."

"Are you going?"

Her mother looked flustered. "Oh, of course not, Angel. I couldn't leave you and Rags, and I couldn't take that much time off from my job and . . ." Mrs. O'Leary's eyes had a faraway look in them.

A car drove up to the curb just then, and Alyce got out and came up the sidewalk. She called out, "Ready to go to the market?"

Alyce drove Mrs. O'Leary to the supermarket every week.

She walked up the steps and patted Angel on the head.

"Mom might go to Canada," Angel blurted out, without knowing why. Alyce always seemed to know everything. This time Angel had heard the news first.

"Angel! Of course I'm not going to Canada. How in the world would I be able to go to Canada?" Mrs. O'Leary explained to Alyce about the phone call.

"Why, that's no problem. I'll move in while you're gone and take care of the children," said Alyce, as if it were all settled. Alyce had recently retired from her job at the department store.

"Oh no, no . . . I couldn't let you do that . . ."

Alyce put her hands out, palms up. "Look," she said. "What's the difference if I live here for a few weeks or at my apartment? I can just settle in here and keep my eye on Angel and Rags and fix their meals — why, we'll have a good time, won't we, Angel?"

Alyce walked over to where Angel sat on the steps and put her arm around her. Hearing the voices above him, Rags came out from under the porch and stood watching with his shovel dangling from one hand.

Angel couldn't picture living with Alyce. She couldn't picture not living with her mother. They had lived together for ten years, nonstop. But she nodded her head.

"Me, too?" said Rags, making sure that he was included in whatever was going on. Small children are so self-centered, thought Angel.

A light that she had never seen before began to gleam in her mother's eyes — an anxious, hopeful look that reminded Angel of the look in the eyes of the puppies at the dog pound when they thought someone was going to take them home. The look told

Angel that her mother needed to go on this trip.

"You need to get away," Alyce chattered on. "When was the last vacation you had?"

"Why," said Mrs. O'Leary. "Not since before I was married, I guess."

"You see? You see?" said Alyce. "Twelve years ago, and you haven't been away alone or without the children since!" Alyce shook her head. "That isn't healthy, you know. Everyone needs a vacation."

Angel wanted to say that she surely could use a vacation from Rags, but she didn't. After all, she had only been with Rags for four years, and her mother had been with her for ten.

"Call her and tell her you'll go," said Alyce. "Call Beth right now."

"I have to go to work," said Angel's mother. "I can't just walk away from my job."

"Don't you have vacation time coming?"

demanded Alyce. "It seems to me you should have all kinds of time accumulated by now."

Angel's mother was about to say something, but Alyce went on. "Call them now and tell them you are using your time off."

They all went inside, and Alyce picked up the phone and handed it to Mrs. O'Leary.

"But the children's dentist appointments and . . ."

"I'll take them to the dentist," said Alyce, shaking the phone at her.

Mrs. O'Leary dialed the number. She explained the situation to the person on the other end. "I can?" she said. "I can take my vacation this month?"

When she hung up, she said, "Mr. Morris said it's a good time, before most people want time off."

"Of course," said Alyce. "Call Beth now and tell her that you'll be ready in a week."

Angel's mother sat down on the couch and put her hand to her chest. "Dear me, I'll

have to think about this. I'll just have to think, you know . . ."

"Sometimes it is best to act first and think later," said Alyce. "If you think too much, you won't do anything."

Angel stored that in her mind for future use. *Act first, think later.*

After a little more urging from Alyce, Mrs. O'Leary called Beth and told her she would go. Angel could hear her aunt's delighted voice on the other end of the phone. "We'll have a wonderful time," she said. "We'll just forget all our worries . . ."

And our children, thought Angel. Her mother would probably forget all about poor Angel and little Rags. She was already heading toward the closet, looking for her suitcase. She and Alyce were babbling on about what clothes to take and what the weather would be like in Canada and how much to tip porters. Her poor children, forgotten so fast. Once her mother was on a plane with Beth, forgetting her worries, she wouldn't give Angel another thought. "Angel?" she'd say. "Angel who?"

Angel went back out on the steps. The day didn't seem as promising now. She felt lonely already, the way an orphan must feel, she imagined. Alyce rushed by, going to the car for a map.

"What's the trouble?" she called, noticing the look on Angel's face. "You want your mother to have a vacation, don't you?"

"Yes, but she could take me along," answered Angel sullenly.

"Then it wouldn't be a vacation," called Alyce, dashing back into the house.

Why wasn't it a vacation with Angel along? Didn't children deserve vacations? Did taking children along mean you couldn't enjoy yourself? For the first time in her life, Angel began to feel like a weight around her mother's neck.

Angel went to the garage and unlocked her bike. She climbed up on it and rode over to Edna's house. Edna was ten, the same age as Angel, and was in the same grade at school. She looked and acted older than Angel, though, since Mrs. O'Leary protected her children more diligently than most mothers.

"I wish my mom would go somewhere," said Edna, when Angel told her about the trip.

"Really?" Angel was surprised. "You want your mom to go away?"

Edna nodded. "I like it when she's gone. I like to be — you know — in charge of things."

"I won't be in charge," said Angel. "Alyce is going to stay with us."

"Still," said Edna, "things are different when your mother's gone. There are different rules and different food — and, well, it's just a good idea to be rid of a mother for a while."

Angel began to feel a twinge of excitement. Maybe Edna was right. After all, she would have to leave her mother some day —

14

when she got married or went to college or left to be a librarian at some big city library. She may as well get used to it now.

"Anyway," said Edna, "she'll probably call you a lot and write all these letters, so you won't really feel that she's away at all. And then before long she'll be back and it will be like she was never gone."

Edna knew so many things. Angel learned a lot from Edna. Last summer at the pool she'd taught her how to pin her locker key inside her swimsuit, and on the first day of school, when Angel had misspelled *conceive,* Edna had taught her the rhyme "*i* before *e* except after *c.*"

The girls rode their bikes to the swimming pool and watched the men cleaning out leaves. But Angel's heart wasn't in it. She could think only of her mother's trip and of how her own life was going to be changed in the following weeks. At noon Angel said goodbye to Edna and rode home.

2

ALYCE MOVES IN

When Angel came to her own block, she could see Alyce unloading unwieldy items from her car and carrying them into the house.

She waved to Angel and called, "I thought I'd move in some things today!"

Angel nodded and parked her bike at the side of the house. Mrs. O'Leary was standing on the porch looking anxious. "Angel," she said. "Where were you? You went off without saying a word."

Before Angel could answer, her mother went on. "Do you think I'm doing the right thing, dear? I mean, will you and Rags be safe and stay out of trouble?"

"Of course," said Angel.

Her mother put her arms around her. "I'll miss you so much," she said.

Rags was at the kitchen table eating cold spaghetti with a spoon. He was kicking the table leg in the annoying way he had and humming a silly nursery rhyme. Mrs. O'Leary walked over and hugged Rags, spaghetti and all. "Oh Rags, I'll miss you so," she said.

Angel thought her mother could afford to miss them. She had a wonderful trip ahead of her and could look forward to all kinds of new experiences. And she could afford to hug Rags, who was covered with tomato sauce and repeating his annoying tune over and over again. She wouldn't see or hear him for ages.

"Rags," called Alyce. "Come and hold the door open for me, dear."

Rags ran to open the door. He stretched himself across it, breathing in to make himself narrow so that Alyce could bring in a dressmaker's dummy, as large as she was, on its metal stand. Alyce was pleasingly plump, Angel's mother always said, not fat.

"You never know. I may get the urge to sew," she said, standing the form in the dining room.

Rags followed Alyce back out to the car and returned carrying a metal plant stand. Alyce was carrying a large rubber plant and a miniature orange tree.

"I have to keep my eye on these," she puffed. "Can't leave them alone in the apartment, you know."

The house was beginning to fill up with Alyce's belongings. She was gingerly moving some of Rags's toys out of the way to make more room.

"I'll bring Tootsie and Bubba and Clarence over at the last minute," said Alyce, sitting down to rest from her efforts.

Angel had forgotten about Alyce's animals. She had a sheep dog named Bubba, a long-haired angora cat named Tootsie, and a yellow canary named Clarence. Of course, they couldn't stay alone in the apartment, either.

"Bubba!" cried Rags.

"Yes, darling, Bubba is going to come and live with Rags! Will you like that?" said Alyce, running her hand through Rags's hair.

Rags nodded his head vigorously. He ran his hand over the back of an imaginary dog. "Nice doggie," he said, petting the air. "Can he sleep with me? In my bed?"

"No," said Angel.

"Yes," said Alyce.

"Maybe," said Angel's mother, all three speaking at the same time.

What were Alyce and her mother thinking of, letting a dog in bed with Rags? Angel wondered what other differences about raising a small boy she and Alyce would have in her mother's absence.

As the time of her vacation grew closer, Mrs. O'Leary's packed suitcases began to collect, one by one, at the back door, waiting. Alyce's belongings gradually took over more and more of the house. Pictures of her relatives stood in bronzed frames on Mrs. O'Leary's dresser. Dog and cat food dishes were placed on paper mats in the kitchen. Her portable sewing machine rested on a card table set up in the dining room beside the dressmaker's dummy. In the freezer were special diet dinners recommended at Alyce's Weight Leaners class, and on the counter were her scale for weighing meat and her wok for making some of the Oriental meals that, she said, were low in calories.

The day Angel's mother's vacation

started, Alyce arrived with her dog, cat, and canary.

"Pretty birdie," sang Rags to Clarence.

"Are we all ready to go?" called Alyce from the doorway.

"Oh my," said Mrs. O'Leary. "I hope I'm doing the right thing."

"Of course you are," said Alyce in a positive voice. "You are going to have the time of your life! And we are too," she added just as positively.

Angel carried her mother's bags out to the car. They were all going along to the airport to see Mrs. O'Leary off.

"Now you help around the house, Angel," said her mother in the car. "Don't let Alyce do all the work. You can help with dinner. And keep your eye on Rags."

Angel nodded her head.

"Rags, you be a good boy."

Rags was busy picking long white cat hairs off his navy blue sweater. He held one up for Angel to see. "Tootsie," he said.

"He'll be a good boy," laughed Alyce from the driver's seat. "Won't you, Rag Bag?" she said, turning around to look at him.

Angel didn't like Alyce's made-up names. And it made her nervous when Alyce looked over her shoulder at the back seat while she was driving. A driver should always keep her eyes on the road. Alyce swerved to miss a milk truck coming onto the freeway. Angel covered her eyes with her hands.

"That guy should look where he's going," said Alyce, angrily beeping the horn.

When they got to the airport, Angel and Rags went with their mother to check in the luggage while Alyce parked the car. Then they walked to Gate 24. Mrs. O'Leary had tears in her eyes.

"I just hope I'm doing the right thing," she said for the fifteenth time that day.

Angel put her arms around her mother's

neck. "Of course you are," she said. "We will take care of everything. Don't worry. Just have a good time and say hello to Auntie Beth for me." Angel thought she sounded very mature, almost adult.

"Kiss," said Rags. Angel's mother hugged Rags very tightly. "Remember, I'll call you as often as I can. You can't write, since we won't be staying in one place."

Just as the passengers began to board the plane, Alyce came running toward them holding a pink rose. She handed it to Mrs. O'Leary, hugging her at the same time. Angel's mother stumbled down the ramp with tears in her eyes, looking over her shoulder and waving the hand holding the rose. Her other hand was clutching the carry-on bag with emergency items that Alyce said she should carry.

Angel pressed her face against the plate glass window and watched the plane take off. It became a little speck in the sky, taking her mother away from her for the first time in her life.

Then she and Rags followed Alyce outside. An emptiness came over her that reminded her of how she had felt on the first day of kindergarten. Something big and familiar and loving was missing. She felt sad all the way to the parking lot. Then she forgot about it when Alyce announced that someone had stolen her car.

"Why would anyone take it?" said Angel, thinking about the rusted headlight and two dented fenders. "Where exactly did you leave it?"

"Right here," said Alyce, pointing to a small open area. No cars were parked there.

Angel looked up at a nearby sign that read No Parking at Any Time.

"I know, but there was no place else to park," Alyce said, and groaned. She sat down on the curb and put her head in her hands. "Dear me, what in the world will we do?" She looked as though she might cry.

"I have to go to the bathroom," said Rags in a whiny voice.

Angel looked at Rags whining and Alyce almost crying. She thought she felt a raindrop on her arm.

"Let's go back into the airport and ask someone about lost cars, and we can take Rags to the rest room."

Alyce cheered up a bit. "That's a good idea," she said.

When they were inside again, Angel saw a booth labeled Information. That was what they needed. "There," she said, pointing. "I'll take Rags to the rest room while you ask."

"Our car is lost," Angel could hear Alyce saying as she went off with Rags.

"Where was it parked?" said the man.

"Right outside, in a place that said No Parking."

When Angel and Rags returned from the rest room, Alyce greeted them with the news, "We have to check the impound lot. Third

25

door down and take the elevator to the ground level."

In the lot Alyce explained the situation to the attendant, all the while dabbing at her eyes with her lace handkerchief and repeating to Rags that everything would be all right.

"License number?" said the man.

Alyce looked through her purse for the license number. Not finding it, she turned her purse upside down on a table and searched through the items, turning them all over, one by one. "I'm afraid I don't know the number," she said.

"Do you have your driver's license?" said the man wearily.

Angel sighed with relief when Alyce produced her driver's license.

The man looked at it and said, "See if you can find the car." He waved his hand toward a long row of delinquent cars. The three of them started down the row.

"Here!" called Rags after a few minutes.

He was a long way down the row. "Here's your car, Alyce."

Alyce ran to Rags and picked him up. She hugged and kissed him over and over. "My little angel!" she crooned. "My little Rag Bag found our car!" She was acting as though Rags had solved all their problems single-handedly.

Alyce eventually found her car keys and opened the door. They climbed in and drove to the exit, where the attendant said, "That will be twenty-seven dollars' towing charge, please."

"Oh my," said Alyce. "I hope I have twenty-seven dollars with me."

Angel was thoroughly disgusted by now. Why in the world didn't Alyce think of this before she parked in a no parking zone? If you are planning to disobey signs, you should at least check to make sure you have enough money to pay any fines. She closed her eyes. She didn't want to hear that Alyce didn't have the money.

"We've got a kitty cat at our house," Rags was telling the attendant. "And a dog and a bird."

The attendant was smiling at Rags with half of his face and frowning with the other half as he waited for the twenty-seven dollars. "That's nice," he said to Rags.

"The bird sings," said Rags, jumping up and down on the seat.

"Will you take a credit card?" asked Alyce in a light voice.

The man shook his head.

"Wait! I'll write a check. That's it. I'll give you a check." A line of cars was forming behind them. After the man found a pen, Alyce wrote a check, and they drove out onto the freeway, free at last.

"Little Rags found our car, yes he did," cooed Alyce on the way home.

Little angel found the car, thought Angel sourly, slumping down in the back seat. She tried not to notice the cars from on-ramps pulling into their lane too close to Alyce.

Angel slept halfway home — until she heard raindrops pelting the roof of the car. Rags soon began to cry. He was afraid of thunder, and at the first few rolls he began whimpering, "I want Mom. I want my mom." Angel put her arm around her brother and soothed him. Maybe her mother's vacation had begun at last, but it looked to her as if anything but a vacation lay in store for the rest of them.

3

STRANGERS COME TO CALL

When Alyce, Angel, and Rags got home from the airport, they found that the windows had been left open and the rain had soaked the furniture and curtains and made water stains on the walls. A few minutes later they discovered that the roast beef, which had been left to thaw on the kitchen counter, was gone. Bubba had eaten it.

"Bad dog!" cried Alyce as Rags petted him. Bubba wagged his tail. "We have to keep the food out of reach," said Alyce.

Angel looked at Tootsie, the white angora cat, sitting on top of the refrigerator, and wondered just where "out of reach" was. Nothing seemed out of reach for these animals.

"And we have to cover the trash," said Alyce, setting a heavy cookie sheet on top of the wastebasket.

After their dinner of tuna fish sandwiches, Angel was surprised to see how late it was. She had to get up early for school in the morning, so she closed all the windows and wiped up the water on the floor as best she could. Then she got Rags ready for bed before going to her own room. As she snuggled down under the covers, the bereft feeling she'd had at the airport returned. Once again, she felt like an orphan. She was too young to be left without a mother. It was a long time before she fell asleep that night.

Angel woke up early in the morning to the smell of something burning. Quickly she dressed for school and ran downstairs to find Alyce frying something thick and brown. It looked like the erasers they used to clean the blackboard at school.

"I'm making French toast," said Alyce brightly, through the smoke that circled her head. "You need a hearty breakfast when you go off to school."

Rags was sitting at the kitchen table in his pajamas, eating marshmallows out of a plastic bag and writing his name on the back of an envelope. Their mother never let them eat candy for breakfast, thought Angel. At this rate, his teeth would all fall out before she returned.

"What's after the *L*?" asked Rags, proud that he was able to print almost his entire name by himself.

"*E*," answered Angel wearily. The whole house was filling up with smoke. The fire department would be coming before long, she was sure.

Alyce set a plate of French toast before Angel. It was black around the edges like a frame and shiny with Karo syrup.

33

Angel tried to think of something she could say that would sound grateful. "We'll make our own breakfast after this," she offered. "We like frozen orange juice and Star Flakes."

Alyce's face and fork fell. She looked disappointed.

"I mean this is good," Angel went on, forcing herself to take a bite out of the middle of the frame, "but I don't really need a big breakfast."

Good heavens, was every meal going to be like this? The house full of smoke and hurt feelings? Alyce had gotten up from the table now and was scrubbing away at the frying pan, which looked as if it was scarred for life.

Rags was feeding his French toast to Bubba, who was under the table. Clarence was singing lustily in his cage in the dining room, and Tootsie was sitting on the stove washing his face. White cat hair wafted in the air with every lick he took.

Angel wondered if she dared go to school.

She was afraid of what she might come home to if she left Alyce alone all day. A lump settled in the pit of her stomach.

"Goodbye," said Angel reluctantly. She gave Rags a big hug and turned to Alyce. "I'll be home exactly at three o'clock." Then she ran off to meet Edna on the playground.

All day at school, Angel tried without success to keep her mind on her work. When her teacher, Miss Peters, asked if something was bothering her, Angel said no. Miss Peters frowned. It was her first year of teaching, and she was very conscientious.

When Angel arrived home at three o'clock, the police were there.

"Alyce couldn't find me," chirped Rags, who was sitting on a policeman's lap, eating a cookie.

Alyce was lying on the sofa with her feet up. A damp cloth was draped across her forehead.

"Why, I looked up and down the block, and then I got into the car and drove all over

town — he was just nowhere in sight . . . I was sure my little Rag Bag had been kidnapped," she was saying. "And me, trusted with these two babies . . . What in the world would their mother say if she came home to find one of them missing?"

"Where were you?" shouted Angel to Rags.

"Under the porch. Where I always am."

"I just never thought of looking under the porch," said Alyce. "I forgot that he spends most of his time there."

"Now if you'll just sign this form," said the policeman who was holding Rags.

Alyce sat up slowly. Her hair was falling out of the bun that it was usually pinned into. She took the pen the officer handed her and signed the form.

"All's well that ends well," the officer said, reassuring them as he put on his hat and waved goodbye.

"I'll get dinner tonight," Angel announced. She was afraid they might have to call the fire department next if Alyce did the cooking.

"Thank you, dear," said Alyce weakly.

Angel walked to the kitchen, angry with her mother all over again. How could she leave them with such an inept sitter? Why didn't Alyce look under the porch? How many times had she come to their house and seen Rags crawl in or out of the latticework with a spade in his hand? How many times had she walked right on that very porch, knowing Rags was beneath it? Maybe it was true what people always said, that you never really know a person until you live with her. Her mother was Alyce's friend, that was true, but she had never lived with her. If she had, Angel was sure, she wouldn't be her friend at all. There was an entirely different woman living here from the one who came to visit and drive Mrs. O'Leary to the market. Angel had always thought that Alyce was a person in control of things.

In the kitchen, Angel discovered that

Alyce had not taken anything out of the freezer to thaw for dinner. Just as she was wondering what to do, there was a knock on the back door.

"Can you get that, Angel?" came Alyce's plaintive voice through the doorway.

Angel opened the door to four total strangers.

"Is Alyce Curdy here?" asked one of the men politely.

"Why, yes, come in," said Angel.

"Who is it, dear?" called Alyce from the couch in the living room.

As soon as she saw the strangers, she exclaimed, "Well, bless my soul, if it isn't Bud and Alma and Hank and Nonnie! And little Myron! Why, how he's changed since the last time I saw him!" One of the men had pushed forward a toddler who had been hiding behind him. From the little boy's shirt pocket, Angel could clearly see the furry head of a real live mouse, complete with whiskers.

Hank helped Alyce up off the sofa and hugged her so hard her feet came off the floor. "How's my Auntie Al?" he said. "My favorite aunt, I always said."

"We went to your apartment when we got to town, and you weren't there!" said the woman called Nonnie. "We wanted to surprise you, but it turned out we were the ones who were surprised!" she added. "Your nice neighbor told us where you were and said, 'You just go right on over there; she'll be real glad to see you.' So here we are! Bud, why don't you bring the bags in. Make yourself useful now, Bud!"

Everyone seemed to think that was a fine joke because they all laughed and laughed and slapped Bud on the back as he went back and forth to the car, bringing four suitcases into the house.

Alyce was on her feet now, nervously pacing from the couch to the door.

"Angel, bring Rags in here and meet my nephews and their wives and little Myron."

Angel walked in slowly, pushing Rags in front of her. She was not used to feeling shy in her own home, but it didn't seem to belong to her anymore.

"So you're an angel, eh?" said Hank, pumping her hand. Hank seemed to be the spokesman for the group — and the comedian. He swung from Angel to Rags, picking him up off the floor and swinging him through the air to his shoulder.

What in the world did Alyce plan to serve these relatives of hers for dinner? And where was she going to put them for the night? And how long were they going to stay? Hank was down on the floor now with Rags, giving him horseback rides.

"Giddap, giddap," shouted Rags, red in the face from all the excitement. Little Myron was now toddling around sprinkling salt as he went, like Hansel and Gretel sprinkling breadcrumbs. Where did he get that saltshaker? He wasn't tall enough to reach the dining room table. Angel noticed that the mouse was no longer in his shirt pocket.

In the middle of the confusion the phone rang. Angel ran to answer it.

"Angel? Angel? Can you hear me? We are in Toronto, darling! Imagine that!"

Angel tried to imagine a place that far away. She'd rather imagine she was there, safe with her mother at the other end of that long wire.

"Is everything all right, Angel? Are you having a good time with Alyce?"

"Everything is fine," lied Angel, though she couldn't bring herself to say that she was having a good time with Alyce.

"Beth and I just had the best dinner in this quaint little place. Oh, Angel, it is marvelous to see new things! But I worry about you all — are you sure you're all right?"

Rags was shouting for the horse to go faster now, and Myron was screaming because someone had taken away his saltshaker and he had just noticed his mouse was missing.

Clarence was singing at the top of his lungs. In the background, Bubba was barking.

"Here he is! Here's your pet!" shouted Bud, scooping the frightened mouse up from under a table.

"It seems awfully noisy there, Angel. What is all that noise?"

Now Bud was putting the mouse back in Myron's pocket. Angel wondered how long he would stay there.

"Alyce has some company, that's all," said Angel. "They came from out of town somewhere. They have a pet mouse," she added.

"Oh, how nice. Can I talk to Rags, Angel?" Angel could tell that her mother's mind was on other things.

Angel put down the phone and pulled Rags off Hank's back. She whispered loudly in his ear, "Mom is on the phone. Don't tell her anything about the police, Rags." She put the phone up to Rags's ear.

"Rags? Is this my Rags? This is your

mother, Rags! Are you all right? Are you having a good time with Angel and Alyce?"

Rags nodded his head vigorously. "Alyce made French toast for breakfast," he said.

"Why, how nice," said Mrs. O'Leary. "You'll be very spoiled by the time I get home!"

Rags handed Angel the telephone and ran off to the horse. Angel felt disgusted with Rags. He seemed to have forgotten about his mother altogether.

Alyce came to the phone and told Mrs. O'Leary what a wonderful time they were having and how good the children were. How could her mother believe all that! Didn't she care about her children at all anymore?

Angel took the phone again to say goodbye. She wanted to keep her mother on the phone a little longer as a kind of link to her old life. But all she heard was the dial tone. Her mother was gone. How were they going to manage? What would Alyce do next?

4

SIRENS BLOW AGAIN

Alyce's relatives went out to Burger Heaven and got hamburgers for everyone. Later that night, although Angel and Rags offered to give up their beds for the night, they insisted on not causing any trouble and slept on the sofa and floor. They put Myron between two chairs on pillows, and two of them even went to Alyce's apartment to sleep.

Angel fell fast asleep in a few minutes. Her last thought before she drifted off was that perhaps she was being too hard on Alyce.

She dreamed that Alyce ran away in the night, leaving Angel a note saying her hair had turned entirely gray overnight and a P.S. saying, "Act now, think later." In the dream, she fled down the street in her nightgown pursued by Angel and Rags (who was promising to be no trouble) and a policeman eating French toast, shouting "All's well that ends well."

She woke up tired from the chase and relieved to find that Alyce was still there, busy in the kitchen making breakfast for everyone. Myron was eating oatmeal with his pet mouse on his lap. Tootsie sat a few feet away, his glance fastened hungrily on the mouse.

By the time Angel came home from school in the afternoon, all the guests had gone and the house was cleaned and swept. Alyce was standing at the stove wearing an apron with the words *Le Chef* printed on it, stirring a pot of homemade spaghetti sauce. The rich, spicy smells filling the air made Angel hungry. She noted with satisfaction that Rags had his hair combed and looked clean. Bubba had a blue bow around his neck. Maybe she'd been right last night after all. Perhaps she had judged Alyce too quickly. How good of her to offer to step into Mrs. O'Leary's shoes and take over for her so that she could have a much-needed vacation. Who else could be so unselfish? Angel scolded herself.

Rags was standing on his head in the dining room.

"We brushed Bubba," he said in a hollow upside-down voice.

"That's nice," said Angel approvingly, although she had already figured that out from the long hair covering Rags's shirt. Alyce was putting a cup of grated carrot into Clarence's cage.

"Angel, Bud called as they were leaving town and said they couldn't find Myron's pet mouse. We looked, Rags and I, and couldn't find him anywhere. Do you have any idea where he might be?"

"I think Tootsie ate him," said Angel.

Alyce stood stock still at these words. They all looked at Tootsie, who was sitting on top of the refrigerator again, washing his face.

"Cats eat mice," said Angel. "It's a known fact." Rags's eyes were big and round.

"Dear me," said Alyce, looking alarmed. She quickly changed the subject. "How was school today?"

"It was the same as always," said Angel truthfully. Then, not wanting to put a damper on the good smells and happy spirit of the afternoon, she added, "Well, perhaps a little better than most days. I was the only one who could spell *extravagant* in the spell-down."

"Why, that's marvelous, dear!"

"I can spell," shouted Rags. "I can write, too. I can write my whole name."

"Of course you can, Rag Bag," said Alyce lovingly.

Rags got his pencil and his old envelope and laboriously copied his name onto the flap.

"The *L* is backward," said Angel.

Rags put his tongue between his teeth and rubbed and rubbed the *L* with his eraser. "There!" he said, printing it correctly. "There's my name!"

Angel nodded. Alyce raved over how smart her little Rag Bag was. Angel was getting awfully tired of hearing how smart and cute Rags was. He was a baby, a pest, that was all. Most little kids were as smart and as cute as he was.

"Dinner is ready!" said Alyce in cheerful tones.

As they ate, Angel felt guilty all over again. The spaghetti tasted delicious, and Alyce had made garlic toast to go with it. It had just taken Alyce a while to settle in, thought Angel. She couldn't be expected to adjust right away. Everything was peaceful now, and that was what mattered. They were almost like a real family. Rags was smiling as he sucked the long noodles into his mouth, one at a time. Of course, Rags looked happy most of the time. He really didn't seem to suffer in a crisis the way she did. He had looked positively delighted when Alyce's boisterous relatives took over.

"I'll do the dishes," said Angel when they had all finished the strawberry shortcake that was dessert.

"Me, too!" shouted Rags.

"No, no, dears. You do your homework, Angel. I'll take care of these dishes in a wink."

"But you cooked the dinner," said Angel. "I think I should do the dishes."

"Shoo. Off with you," said Alyce, waving Angel out of the room with the dish towel.

Angel reluctantly went into the living room and got out her school books. She could hear Alyce rattling the dishes and singing along with the radio. Clarence was singing at the top of his lungs, too. Rags followed Angel a moment later and sat under the dining room table to play with his miniature cars.

Angel tried to remember how much seven times nine was and couldn't. It made her sleepy just to think of it. She was considering making a long list of nines and adding them up when her head fell to the table and she dozed off.

Suddenly an enormously loud crash in the other room woke her up. Or had she been dreaming? Had the crash happened in her sleep? She had just decided that this was the case and closed her eyes again when she heard the screams.

"HELP!" she heard. "Angel, Rags, HELP!"

Angel stumbled to her feet and flew through the dining room to the kitchen. Rags was just coming out from under the dining room table as she passed. He stood up so swiftly that the tablecloth came up with him, covering his head and sending the full sugar bowl and creamer as well as Alyce's fresh flower centerpiece to the floor with another crash.

When they got to the kitchen, Angel stopped in horror. Alyce was flat on the floor, clutching a broken platter to her chest. Beside her was a kitchen chair on its back, one of its legs broken. Angel wanted to look away; it didn't seem right to look at Alyce in such a vulnerable position, all spread out beneath them. Even Rags with the tablecloth still over his head seemed to be more in control of the situation than Alyce. The cupboard doors yawned open over their heads.

"I don't know how it happened," said Alyce in a voice that seemed to come from a long way off. "I couldn't reach the top shelf where the platter belongs, so I stepped on the chair . . ." Their eyes all followed hers to the chair on its back. "And all of a sudden it went out from under me — I must have been standing too close to the edge — and down I went."

Angel and Rags stood speechless, rooted to the same spot.

"Get up, Alyce," said Rags, breaking the silence. "Get up." Rags made upward motions with his small hands.

"I'm afraid I can't move," moaned Alyce. "Something seems to be — broken."

Angel knew that she should have done the dishes. If she had done the dishes none of this would have happened. Oh why did she listen to Alyce?

"Ooooohhhhh," moaned Alyce again from the floor. "My leg . . . It feels terrible."

"Get up, Alyce," said Rags again, crying now himself. "Get up!"

Angel stamped her foot. "She can't get up, Rags! Something is broken."

"Alyce is broken. Alyce is broken!" Rags was crying even louder.

Angel remembered reading that people sometimes had a sudden flow of strength in a

crisis. Something in their sympathetic nervous systems took over and gave them the strength to move mountains — well, at least to lift things like cars. Perhaps, with Rags's help, she could lift Alyce.

"Let's move her to the couch," Angel said to Rags. "Come and help me."

"Alyce is broken," whimpered Rags, now cowering in the corner of the kitchen.

"Don't panic, Alyce," said Angel. "We'll just get you onto the couch where you'll feel better."

Angel tried to lift Alyce. She didn't move. Then Angel tried to drag her. She still didn't move. Angel didn't feel any strength at all. She must not have one of those sympathetic nervous systems, she thought. Alyce moaned softly once more.

"Call the doctor, dear," whispered Alyce. "Just call the doctor."

"Yes! Yes, don't worry, Alyce. I'll get the doctor."

Angel ran to the phone. She took down the little blue book where her mother kept emergency numbers and leafed through the pages until she found her doctor's number. But when she dialed the number, a recording answered. It said that office hours were over for the day.

"The hospital!" said Angel. "I'll call the hospital."

She dialed a second time and spoke to someone at the hospital who said that an ambulance would be sent right out.

"With a stretcher," said Angel with authority. "We'll need a stretcher." When she hung up, she noticed that her hands were sweating.

Angel ran back to Alyce and knelt beside her. "They're coming," she said. "Don't worry about a thing."

Alyce's face was whiter than she'd ever thought anyone's face could be, and her eyes were closed. She didn't answer.

Rags came up behind Angel and said, "Maybe she's dead."

"Of course she's not dead," said Angel impatiently. But just to be sure, she felt Alyce's wrist the way she'd seen doctors do in movies.

"I can feel her pulse," she said, reassured at the discovery.

"Alyce's eyes are closed. Alyce is dead," Rags insisted.

"She's not dead!" Angel hissed between her teeth. "Now go clean up that sugar and stuff from the floor before the ambulance gets here."

"Oh my, such a burden," said Alyce, slowly opening her eyes. "I'm such a burden."

"Of course you aren't," Angel lied.

"And what will become of you children?" wailed Alyce. "Oh my little Rag Bag and my Angel . . . How can you get along without me?"

"We'll be fine," said Angel, thinking that it was easy enough to take care of themselves. It was Alyce herself who was the problem.

Alyce seemed to lapse into another faint. Angel put a pillow from the couch under her head and covered her with a blanket. She had heard that people in accidents got chilled easily. Then, not knowing what else to do, she helped Rags clean up the sugar and cream and flowers and broken glass from the floor.

If she didn't do something to keep busy, the panic in her stomach would take over, and what would Rags do if she went to pieces?

Just then, an ambulance, siren screaming and red lights flashing, came down the street. Rags began jumping up and down. At the same time, Clarence began to sing shrilly, and Bubba began to bark. Alyce was moaning softly.

The ambulance attendants came up the

porch steps carrying oxygen tanks, stretchers, and blankets. The ambulance stood at the curb, lights still flashing. A police car and a fire engine soon joined it, and a crowd began to gather on the lawn.

"Where's the victim?" said a deep voice.

"In the kitchen," Angel said, pointing.

More men came to the door, one of them carrying an axe. When he saw that there was no fire, he positioned himself at the door, holding it open for the stretcher to go through.

Angel and Rags stood watching, motionless, while the men loaded Alyce onto the stretcher and carried her out the back door and down the steps to the ambulance. As they transferred her to a cot in the back, she called out anxiously, "Angel, call Margaret Toomer. Ask her to come and stay while I'm gone. And have the left-over spaghetti for dinner tomorrow and lock the doors and . . ." Alyce's voice trailed off as the ambulance doors closed.

Rags and Angel stood on the lawn and watched the ambulance drive away. Through the window, they saw Alyce, a pleading look in her eye, mouthing some directions to them.

5

RAGS GOES TO SCHOOL

Angel and Rags watched the ambulance drive down the street and turn the corner on the way to the hospital. The crowd began to disperse, and the children returned to the house. It was as quiet now as a church. Someone had turned the radio off, and Clarence was standing on one foot in his cage with his head under his wing, asleep. Bubba and Tootsie were both curled up on the couch. The excitement must have tired them, thought Angel. She looked at the furniture, pushed out of the way for the stretcher, and at the kitchen, which showed all the signs of the accident: the open cupboards, the broken chair, the sofa pillow where Alyce's head had lain. Angel shivered. The whole house had the air of a place after a party ends abruptly.

"Alyce is broken," whined Rags, back to his earlier lament now that the frenzy of sirens and flashing lights was past.

"She isn't broken," said Angel crossly. "Not all of her, anyway. She'll get fixed at the hospital. Let's get this stuff in order."

"Alyce will get fixed," sang Rags as they put dishes away and got the house back to normal. "What will they fix her with, Angel? Glue?" Here Rags giggled, picturing Alyce glued together.

Angel was in no mood to laugh. She did, however, feel a degree of relief that Alyce was safe in the hospital. She couldn't possibly get into trouble there.

Angel fed the animals so that she wouldn't have to do it in the morning before school, and then she remembered that she was supposed to call Margaret Toomer, who lived across the street. Rags would have to have someone to stay with while Angel was in school. She went to the phone and dialed the number. The phone rang and rang. No one answered. Angel hung up and dialed again. She let it ring twenty times. Still no answer. Well, she'd call in the morning when she got up. Margaret would surely be there in the early morning.

"Alyce broke herself in two. She's getting all fixed up with glue," sang Rags as Angel washed him up and helped him into his pajamas. Rags liked to make things rhyme. Their mother said that was because he was very creative. He might be a poet or songwriter when he grew up, she said, although Angel couldn't picture Rags as a poet. Her mother never said things like that about her. Probably because Angel never had time to be creative, she was so busy taking care of Rags and his disasters.

With her brother finally tucked in for the night, Angel went to her own room and got ready for bed herself. She was sure that with all the excitement of the day she would go right to sleep, but instead she lay in bed wide awake. This was the first time she had ever been alone with Rags in the house overnight. They were real orphans, all alone in a big house, responsible for themselves at such an early age. The more Angel thought about it, the more she felt like crying.

After a while, she began to wonder about Alyce in the hospital. Here she had mixed feelings. Poor Alyce, she thought, in pain and no doubt worrying about the children she had promised to take care of. On the other hand, what a stupid thing to do, to climb up on a chair and risk death by falling on her head. How selfish of Alyce to risk dying, leaving Angel and little Rags alone.

Angel's thoughts were interrupted by a squeaky noise. It seemed to come from overhead, in the attic. While she strained her ears for more squeaks, she thought she heard another noise, a sort of rustling. Was it the wind? She remembered that the furnace sometimes made strange noises. But the furnace wasn't on now — was it? She lay quiet and stiff under her blanket, afraid to move. Dear me, there were all kinds of noises in the house. She never remembered hearing them when her mother was home. Or even when Alyce had been here. Could it be the active imagination her mother spoke of? Could a person's imagination make things happen?

Bravely, she crept out of bed and tiptoed across the hall to check on Rags. He was sleeping blissfully, apparently without a care in the world. Angel felt like stamping her foot and waking him up to insist that he worry along with her. It was awful to be the only one awake in a big old house, in the middle of the night, with something lurking in the attic, or maybe the basement, waiting to pounce on them. Then she thought of Rags crying and whining and decided she was better off with him asleep.

Maybe she should leave the bathroom light on. And maybe the hall light, too. She flicked the light switches on and crept back to bed, pulling the covers over her head.

There it was again! The noise was closer this time. It was a brushing kind of noise, like something moving right over her head. Whoever was in their house was upstairs now, maybe right in her own room! Angel could hear her heart beating. She sat up in bed and tried to make out familiar objects in the dark. Moonlight lit the outside brightly enough so that she could see that all the houses around hers were dark. Everyone was sleeping in a burglar-free — or a ghost-free — house, except her. Could it really be a ghost? Which would be better, she wondered, a burglar or a ghost?

"I have to arm myself," Angel whispered. She crept out of bed for the second time and went to her closet. As she opened the door, a coat hanger fell to the floor. No. That wasn't a good weapon. She felt along the shelves and came to a box of paper dolls. That was no good. Neither was her old doll stroller, folded up on the floor. There were her roller skates — she'd forgotten about them. What was that behind the skates? Her umbrella! That might make a good weapon.

She took her red umbrella with the white ducks marching around the rim out of the closet and set it by her bed. She wouldn't go looking for trouble, but if trouble came to her, she had a weapon to use in self-defense.

Angel saw by her bedside clock that it was after midnight, a ghostly hour. Feeling a bit safer with a weapon by her side, she closed her eyes and tried to relax her stiff muscles. She tried to think of how this burglar (or ghost) had gotten in. She was sure she had remembered to lock the doors downstairs. But of course, a ghost didn't need a door — it could come right through a wall.

Angel tossed and turned. She looked at her clock again and saw that it was two-thirty in the morning! It would soon be time to get up to go to school. By four-thirty she was asleep. She dreamed that she and Rags were chasing a ghost wearing a plaster cast on its leg. It had a face like Alyce's.

After a brief, fitful sleep, Angel woke up tired to a loud knock at the door. She looked at her clock and saw that it was eight-thirty, time to leave for school, and she hadn't even eaten breakfast or dressed yet!

She ran past Rags's room, where he lay sleeping peacefully, and down the stairs to the back door.

"Edna!" she said as she unlatched the safety chain. "It's good you came or I would have slept right through school."

Edna looked like she had had a good night's sleep and a healthy breakfast. And a loving mother had French braided her hair and tied crisp blue ribbons in it. Angel was suddenly very conscious of standing before her friend barefoot, in a nightgown with a hole in it. But she was too tired and hungry to care.

"Come in, Edna," Angel said, and yawned. "I have to eat breakfast and get dressed. And I have to find someone to stay with Rags."

While Angel poured some cornflakes into a bowl, she told Edna the whole story, including the noises she had heard the night before. Edna sat gingerly on the edge of a chair and listened.

"Boy," she said, "nothing like that ever happened when my mother went out of town."

Angel put her empty bowl in the sink and ran to the telephone to call Margaret Toomer. As it had the night before, the phone rang and rang.

"She *has* to be home this morning," said Angel impatiently. She let it ring some more.

Then she dialed the number over and let it ring again.

"Where could she be?" said Angel, angry now.

"Probably out of town," said Edna. "Didn't you tell me that she goes to visit her daughter in Madison sometimes?"

Angel hung up the phone. Edna must be right. What in the world was she going to do with Rags?

"We're going to be late," said Edna, looking at her little gold wristwatch.

"Maybe you better go ahead. There's no use our both being late."

Edna sensed an element of adventure here and weighed it against the repercussions of being late. "I'll wait for you," she said. "You might need help — getting Rags a place to stay and stuff."

"There is no place for Rags to stay," said Angel, leading Edna upstairs, where she began to dress. "At least, no place I can find

70

this morning before school." Her voice was muffled as she pulled her skirt over her head.

"We could leave him at my house, except that my mom just left for the city. Her bridge tournament is today. But don't worry. There has to be some solution," continued Edna.

"I know what you can do!" she said a moment later to the bathroom door, behind which Angel was running water and brushing her teeth.

"What?" called Angel. "Talk louder, Edna, I can't hear you."

"I said I have an idea," shouted Edna. "Why don't you take Rags along to school? That would solve everything."

Angel opened the bathroom door. She stood, with her toothbrush in her hand, looking doubtfully at Edna.

Edna quickly added, "Remember when we were in second grade? Polly Randall brought her little sister to school a lot."

It would certainly solve one problem, thought Angel. But knowing Rags, it would only lead to new ones. Still, it was late, and she didn't have much choice. She had to do something immediately.

Edna was already down the hall calling Rags to get out of bed. By the time Angel got there, Edna was going through his dresser drawers looking for navy blue socks to match the T-shirt she had found. She found them and helped him to pull them on.

"I have to wash," said Rags, not used to being hurried out of his pajamas so quickly.

"You got washed last night," said Angel. "We're in a hurry, Rags. You're going to school with us today."

"School?" said Rags, his eyes opening wide at the word.

Angel ran to the bathroom and wet a comb to slick Rags's hair back, while Edna got his jacket from the closet and put his arms in the sleeves.

"I can do it!" said Rags crossly. Edna tied his tennis shoes, and the children ran down the stairs and out the back door.

"I didn't have breakfast!" wailed Rags.

The girls looked at each other. They had forgotten that Rags needed to eat.

Edna opened her lunch box and reached inside. She took out an orange and two brownies. "Here," she said. "This will keep you till lunch time."

"I forgot about lunches, too," said Angel, running along beside Edna. "We'll have to come home and eat some cold spaghetti."

"You're sure lucky to be in charge of everything," said Edna enviously. "I'd like to eat cold spaghetti and stay alone all night. It must be great not having anyone telling you what to do all the time."

Angel stared at Edna. She couldn't be serious. Why would she want to be scared to death all alone or be awake all night hearing noises and have a little brother trailing her to school who would probably embarrass her (in some way, she didn't know how just yet) and come home from school to cold left-over noodles instead of a nice hot dinner and the smell of cookies baking? Doing a few errands for her mother was a small price to pay for freedom from worry. And that was all Angel seemed to be doing these days, worrying about one thing after another.

"Ha," she said to Edna. "You're just saying that."

"No, really. I'd love it," said Edna emphatically.

"What do I tell Miss Peters?" said Angel as they got to the classroom door. All the other children were in their seats already, taking out their social studies books.

"Just tell her the truth — he has no place to stay," said Edna. "I'll tell her for you."

When they opened the door, twenty-four heads turned to watch them enter. Ignoring the stares of her classmates, Edna walked right up to the teacher's desk and said, "This is Rags. Caroline has no one to take care of him, so she had to bring him to school."

Edna was brave, Angel had to admit that. Of course, she thought, if it had been Edna's little brother here, Angel wouldn't be embarrassed either. By now, Edna had taken her seat, and everyone's attention was focused on Angel and Rags.

"Open your books and read chapter six," said Miss Peters to the class. Then she said in a low voice to Angel, "Perhaps you had better tell me what happened."

Angel told Miss Peters about her mother's trip and added that Alyce had been called away on an emergency.

"When will she be back?" said Miss Peters.

"Oh, very soon," said Angel. Angel could see some questions forming in Miss Peters's mind and a frown over her eyes. If Angel told her the truth, Miss Peters might be

75

alarmed. She might even put them in a foster home. (Angel had heard about such things happening.) She'd be a real orphan then and perhaps never see her mother again.

"She'll be home by the time we get out of school today," said Angel, taking no chances.

"I see," said Miss Peters, looking relieved. "Well, Rags is welcome here with us. Why don't you just pull one of the little chairs up to your desk so that he can sit with you and not be shy."

Miss Peters patted Rags on the head with one hand and waved a chair over with the other. Everyone stared at Rags. Overcome with the new experience, Rags sat motionless for the next half-hour. "I'm in school," he repeated over and over under his breath, savoring this occasion to the fullest. Everyone, including Angel, seemed very large to him. He was a dwarf in a room of giants and giants' furnishings. Rags watched carefully as the giants waved their hands. This meant you could talk, Rags soon learned. No one talked without first waving a hand in the air.

"Now who would like to give his social studies report on city workers?" Miss Peters was saying.

Dozens of hands went up. Miss Peters called on a boy named Andrew. He walked to the front of the room and began to tell the class about the responsibilities of the police chief.

Just as Andrew was well launched on his subject, Rags waved both hands in the air and walked to the front of the room still waving them. He stood beside Andrew, with his arms above his head, and said, "The policeman came to our house."

There wasn't a sound in the room. Everyone was motionless, including Miss Peters and Angel. It all happened so fast that no one knew quite what to do — yet.

Rags looked at his audience. He had their attention. "Twice," he said. "Twice they came to our house." Here Rags held up two of his fingers on one of his waving hands.

"The red lights were flashing and the sirens were on — o-o-oo-h! — and the police car pulled up by our curb, and the police-man got out of his police car and ran up the steps and into our dining room!"

Angel felt the foster home becoming more of a reality every minute.

Rags went on. "Then another police car came and then ambulances and fire trucks! Three of them." Here Rags took his hand down and lifted three fingers up and then returned his hand to the air. "And a man with an axe," said Rags.

It was still quiet in the room.

Finally the silence was broken by Miss Peters, who said uncertainly, "Rags, that is a very fine story indeed, but it is Andrew's turn to speak to the class."

"My hands are up," said Rags, standing his ground, his feet firm and his shoulders back.

"Nevertheless, you will have to sit down. It is Andrew's turn."

Rags realized that Miss Peters didn't believe his story. She probably thought he had made it all up. Rags struggled to keep from bursting into tears. Miss Peters's voice sounded harsh, as if he had done something wrong on his first day of school. He had done what the others had done, and it was wrong. It wasn't fair. Rags wasn't sure he wanted to come back, not if teachers were so unkind.

A tear ran down Rags's face. Miss Peters came to the front of the room and put her arm around him, at the same time leading him gently toward Angel's desk. As if a dam had burst, the whole class broke into laughter. Angel's face turned bright red, and she stared out the window trying not to look at anyone, especially Miss Peters. Now Rags was sobbing in earnest. The big kids were all laughing at him.

"Class!" said Miss Peters in her harsh voice. "Rags did not know any better. We don't laugh when people make mistakes, do we?"

The laughing subsided to giggles, then to a sort of buzz, and then it was quiet.

"Go ahead, Andrew," said Miss Peters.

Rags's sobs were quiet now. There was only a sniffle now and then, and a shaking of his shoulders, as he hunched over Angel's desk.

While Andrew was speaking, Miss Peters got a large piece of paper and a pencil and gave it to Rags. When he saw it, he rubbed his red eyes and said "Thank you." He felt friendlier now toward the teacher. He loved paper and pencils. He loved to write his name and draw. This was what school was supposed to be. A place to use paper and pencils.

Angel was relieved that no one thought Rags's story was true. Rags busied himself immediately writing *Rags O'Leary* painstakingly down one margin of the paper and up the other. When he had filled one sheet on both sides, Miss Peters slipped another sheet onto his desk. When he finished that, another sheet appeared. The class finished social studies and went on to math. Then they had reading and spelling, and still Rags wrote. His arm was growing stiff, and his fingers were getting red from holding the pencil so tightly. School was hard work. But Rags expected that. He wasn't a lazy person.

Now Rags was really tired. He wondered how many more sheets of paper Miss Peters expected him to fill. He thought of taking a rest, but he didn't want the teacher to think he was too small to keep up with the big kids. He began to draw police cars and fire trucks. Angel gave him her crayons and he colored his pictures. And then at last it was recess time.

"What a darling little brother," said one of the girls on the playground. Soon a group gathered around Angel and Rags and Edna, everyone making a fuss over Rags. Angel forgot some of her embarrassment of the morning.

"Where did you get those big brown eyes?" cooed one of the girls.

"Look how he can write his name already!" said another, looking at one of Rags's papers.

Rags didn't like this kind of attention. It made him feel like a baby.

"Angel," he said, "can I stay out on the playground after you go in?"

The children laughed. "Tired of school already?" one of them said. Rags wished they'd all go away.

Angel thought that was a good idea. There were swings and sandboxes and slides out here, all kinds of things for Rags to keep busy with. And if he wasn't in the classroom he couldn't embarrass her.

"I'll ask Miss Peters," she promised.

The bell rang and the children went back into the school. Angel came out in a while and said yes, Rags could stay on the playground if he didn't get into any trouble. Miss Peters was at the window, frowning. She looked like she wasn't sure she'd made the right decision.

"And don't go away," said Angel firmly. "I'll come and get you in one hour, and we'll go home for lunch."

Rags nodded. He was glad to be free for an hour from filling up those papers. It was quiet on the playground now. Singing came from one of the open school windows. A breeze blew over the treetops, and the warm sun felt good on Rags's bare head.

There were too many people in Angel's room, thought Rags. It was nice out here with lots of space and no one laughing at him. Rags slid down the slide. He climbed up again and went down backward. Then he climbed to the top of the jungle gym. From this height, he could see almost to his own house. He could see the top of the hospital where Alyce lay broken. And he could see two men putting new cement down in front of the school for a new sidewalk. A truck with a long spout poured the wet cement into a big pile. The men were smoothing it into place with something that looked like a rake.

Rags got down from the jungle gym and walked to the front of the school. He sat down on the grass beside the truck to watch the men. The cement looked wet and inviting, like something that would be fun to walk barefoot in. *Slush, slush,* it went as the men worked. I'll bet it's like modeling clay, thought Rags. If he had a big handful, he could probably make a dog or a bird or a police car. It would get hard and become a statue. Rags thought of all the things he could do with cement if he had some.

Finally the truck stopped spouting cement. The men smoothed the newly laid sidewalk into a glossy finish with big trowels. They put up a sawhorse at each end and signs that read Wet Cement.

Then one of the men looked at his watch and said, "Let's quit for lunch, Charlie." The other one nodded and picked up the tools. Then they both loaded them into the back of another truck and drove away.

Rags sat for a long time looking at the smooth, wet cement. He wanted to walk in it with bare feet, but he had a feeling Angel would be cross. It probably wouldn't come off his feet with water.

Rags picked up a stick that was lying on the grass and began to peel the bark off it. Maybe he should put a little mark in one corner of the cement so that years later, when he was an old man, he could come back and see it. No other kids had something of theirs in cement. Rags had seen words in cement on sidewalks. Words like *Ace Cement Co.* Maybe he could make his handprint. He walked up to the sidewalk and tested it with one finger. Just as he thought, nice and squishy, perfect for a handprint. He placed his hand, palm down, in the corner. It felt cold and good. But when he took it up, he could hardly see any mark.

"I guess that's not enough," he said softly. "Maybe I should make an *R* for *Rags*."

He took his stick and wrote a small *R*. Then he stood back to look at it. He couldn't see it at all unless he was right up close to it. It should be a little bigger, thought Rags.

He smoothed the small *R* out and made a large *R*. Then he wrote an *A* and then *GS*. It looked beautiful! Now everyone would know that Rags could write, even if he was just a little boy. The *RAGS* looked so good that he wrote *O'LEARY* after it. Then, to balance things out, he wrote it in the other corners, too. But there was all that space in the middle, just begging to be written on. Smooth, smooth, glassy cement. What difference did it make if people walked on a smooth sidewalk or a rough one? None, thought Rags. And while they were walking, they'd look down and read his name. "Oh, I know Rags O'Leary," they'd say. "I didn't know he

could write though!" It would give them something entertaining to do while they were just walking along, probably bored. Rags hated to be bored. Angel did, too. She would be glad to see a sidewalk that wasn't boring.

By the time the lunch bell rang, the sidewalk wasn't boring anymore. "It looks beautiful!" sang Rags as he ran back to the jungle gym to wait for Angel. He felt warm inside just thinking of all those people who would read his name for years and years to come.

"There he is!" shouted Edna as the children poured out onto the playground. "Right where we left him."

"I'm glad you didn't get into any trouble," said Angel. "Let's go home and eat."

6

WET CEMENT

When Angel and Rags opened their back door, the phone was ringing. Angel had begun to dread the sound of the phone lately. There was always the chance that it might be her mother. She didn't want to evade her mother's questions, but she surely didn't want her to learn about all the disasters going on at home, either, and have to rush back. If this vacation was spoiled, she'd have to take another, and Alyce would move in again for no telling how long the next time.

Angel picked up the telephone gingerly. "Hello?" she said.

"Angel?" said a voice that was not her mother's. "How are you, Angel, and how is my dear little Rag Bag?"

"Alyce!" said Angel. "How are you?"

"Angel, I'm going to be fine. They took x-rays and only my leg is broken. Wasn't I lucky?"

Angel didn't think it was lucky to have a broken leg, but she agreed with Alyce because Alyce was a grown-up and must know what is lucky and what isn't.

"I only have to be here for another day, and then I will be home again with you and Rags! The doctor said, 'Alyce, you can mend at home just as well as you can mend in the hospital' — such a nice man. And I said, 'I just have to get home to my responsibilities. I just can't leave those children.' And he said he understood, and after all I could mend at home just as well as in the hospital . . ." Alyce's voice trailed off into a story about her leg being one of the worst they had ever x-rayed, and about the food in the hospital having too many calories, and about how she couldn't eat anyway just thinking of the children without her ... "Did you get Margaret to come over, Angel?" she asked.

Angel was just about to tell Alyce that Margaret Toomer was out of town when she caught herself. Who knew what Alyce would do if she found out that the children were alone. She might send them to a foster home herself. Or she might have a relapse and be in the hospital for weeks. Or, worst of all, she might call the police again and have them track down her mother somewhere in Canada. (Angel could picture the mounted police she'd seen in movies flying over mountains and streams to her mother, who would probably faint at the news.) No, the truth, which until last week had been the most natural thing in the world to her, was now impossible.

Angel pondered sadly on how telling one

little lie led to so many more. It was all so complicated. But she was trapped.

"Angel?" said Alyce again. "Margaret is there, isn't she?"

"Yes," sighed Angel. "She's here."

"Good," said Alyce. "Maybe I should . . . Oh Angel, dear, here is the nurse to take my blood pressure. I'll be home tomorrow. Can you manage one more day? For dinner tell Margaret there are my Weight Leaners dinners in the freezer — three of them. They're perfectly nutritious. You can make a green salad to go with them. Use the lettuce and tomato in the refrigerator."

Angel heard the nurse rattling her equipment in the background. She said goodbye and hung up the phone.

Angel heated up the cold spaghetti for lunch. Rags stirred it around his dish while it got later and later.

"Eat!" said Angel crossly.

"I won't!" said Rags, pushing it away.

Angel made up her mind never to have

children. "I don't care. You can just go hungry," she said, and gave the spaghetti to Bubba. Then she felt guilty and made Rags a peanut butter sandwich and some toaster-waffles. On the way back to school they munched stalks of wilted celery that had been in the refrigerator too long. Edna met them at the corner as they were ready to cross the street to the school. A crowd had gathered in front of the building. When the bell rang, the three children ran to the playground and got into line.

In the classroom Rags sat down in his little chair at Angel's desk just as if he had been coming to school all year. It was already beginning to feel a little boring to him. When Miss Peters slipped him another piece of paper, Rags sighed audibly and began to fidget.

"Cut that out. Just draw something," whispered Angel. "Or write your name."

It had been fun to write his name in the morning. It wasn't fun anymore. Rags didn't care if he never wrote his name again. Walking back to school, he had wanted to tell Angel about the excitement of writing his name in wet cement, but something had stopped him. He himself knew it was a fine thing to do, but something deep inside told him Angel might not think so. He had better keep it his own little secret for now.

Rags began to copy the words from Angel's speller. These were new words anyway, big words he'd never seen before. He worked hard, and by two o'clock he had fifteen words in a row on his paper. The class had just finished music class and was busy reading library books. It was quiet in the room with everyone reading peacefully and Miss Peters correcting papers at her desk. Rags leaned back and stretched. He was tired. School was a lot of work, no doubt about it.

As he picked up his pencil to begin again, there was an announcement on the public address system. Angel had told many stories at home about how people who were in trouble were called to the office on the PA system by the principal. Sometimes other messages were given, like when school closed early for a teachers' meeting.

"Your attention please!" shrieked the PA system. Then there was a low whistling sound. Everyone sat up to listen to the report. Maybe the principal was going to announce an upcoming fire drill, and they would get to go outside and stand in the sun and pretend that the school was burning down.

"Your attention please!" repeated the system. More whistling. "If there is someone in this school by the name of — uh — Rags, yes, that's it, Rags O'Leary, will he or she please come to the office immediately. Your attention please! Will Rags O'Leary please come to the office! Thank you!"

Every head in the room turned toward Angel's desk. Angel herself could not believe her ears. How in the world did they even know Rags's name? And why would they want Rags anyway? He wasn't even enrolled in the school! A feeling in her stomach told her that Rags was in some sort of school trouble that he had somehow managed to hide from her.

Out of the silence that followed the message, Miss Peters managed to say, "Caroline, would you please take Rags to the office?"

Angel started for the door with Rags, feeling every eye in the room on them.

"Why would they want you?" said Angel as soon as they were out in the hall.

Rags raised his shoulders in a gesture that said he didn't know. "Why would they?" he repeated. "Maybe they want to give me a present or something," he added.

"They don't even know you, Rags. How would they even know you're here today?"

"Maybe Miss Peters told them," said Rags wisely. "Or Edna."

When they got to the office, the woman behind the desk, who looked very tall to

Rags, said to Angel, "Are you Rags O'Leary?" with surprise in her voice. She sounded as if she never expected to meet anyone named Rags O'Leary, even though it was a name announced to the whole school just a moment ago.

"He is," said Angel, pointing to Rags.

"I am," said Rags expectantly, his chin just coming to the top of her file cabinet. He still had a present in mind.

"Come this way," said the woman, leading them into the office of the principal, Father Ryan.

"This is Rags O'Leary," the woman said. Angel thought she saw her smile.

The principal was not smiling. "Sit down," he said to the children.

Then he leaned back in his big leather chair that swiveled and said, "So you are Rags O'Leary."

Hadn't the woman in the office just said that he was? Angel thought this was already very clear.

"Do you go to school here?"

Angel repeated the story she had told to Miss Peters that morning. The principal kept nodding as she talked.

"I see," he said finally. He swiveled around in his chair and faced Rags. "It seems that someone," he said, "we don't know who, has written your name in the wet cement in the sidewalk in front of the school, and . . ."

"Not someone," said Rags proudly, interrupting Father Ryan. "It was me."

"It was you," repeated Father Ryan. "Well, ah, Mr. O'Leary. The cement was quick-setting cement, and by the time the workmen returned from their lunch and discovered the damage, it was too late for them to remove the marks."

"Not damage." Rags pouted. "My name."

"Yes — ah — well, it's all in how you look at it, isn't it? At any rate, the sidewalk has to be redone, at some cost to the school. More cement, more labor . . . You see," the principal went on, "in cases of — er — vandalism like this, we expect restitution to be made."

Angel felt herself growing angry. Rags might be many things, but he was no vandal. He would not deliberately ruin a sidewalk. Of course, she hadn't actually seen it yet, but she did know Rags was no vandal. It made her angry that this man had implied her brother was a common hoodlum. Then the full realization of what he was saying hit her.

"You mean we have to pay?" said Angel.

"Yes," said Father Ryan. "It's the only way youngsters learn to take responsibility for their actions."

Now it sounded like Rags was a delinquent. It was a good thing her mother was away. Why, if she heard Father Ryan calling Rags a juvenile delinquent there was no telling what she'd do!

"How much money is it?" asked Angel.

"Well, the whole job will probably cost well over one hundred dollars, getting the truck out again and all. But we expect the offenders" (he spoke as if Rags wrote on sidewalks every day) "to pay only a part of the cost, say, twenty-five dollars in this case. We generally suggest that they earn the money themselves, so that they learn their lesson, so to speak."

Rags was humming a tune under his breath and playing with the knobs on the principal's desk. He wasn't even paying attention to what they were saying.

Father Ryan looked doubtfully down at him. "Perhaps Rags here is too young to know better, but since you brought him to school, the responsibility would fall on you as well."

Angel felt mixed emotions again. She was partly angry at Rags for causing trouble and partly angry at Father Ryan for blaming her for what had happened.

Father Ryan stood up, as if that was all he had to say. "Since you say no one's home at the moment, I'll call your house on Monday to discuss the matter with your sitter," he said, walking them to the office door.

"We'll take care of it. We'll pay the money," said Angel.

"I think," said the principal as they were going out the door, "that the gravity of this situation should be impressed upon your little brother, so that no more unfortunate episodes occur in the future."

"It will," said Angel.

When they got out in the hall, Angel shook Rags by the shoulders. "Why did you write in the cement?" she said. "Why did you do something so dumb?"

"It looked nice," said Rags. "It isn't dumb."

"Show me where you did it," demanded Angel.

Rags led Angel out the front door to the new sidewalk. "It was just plain before," said

102

Rags, pointing. "Now it's fancy. People can read my name on it," he added proudly.

"Well, they aren't going to read your name," said Angel crossly. "They have to put a whole new sidewalk in."

"Take my name away?" screamed Rags. "Are they going to take my name away?"

"Yes, and we have to pay them to do it."

At the thought of all of his hard work and his good name erased, Rags burst into tears. "I want my name here." He lay down on the grass and pounded his fists on the ground.

"You get up this minute and stop crying," said Angel, stamping her foot and meaning business. "It was wrong to write on someone else's sidewalk. It isn't yours, Rags."

"Well, it's my name, and I don't want anybody to take it away," said Rags, crying harder than ever.

The recess bell rang just then, and the other children came out to play. When they saw Angel and Rags, they came over to see what Rags had done.

"When could he have done it?" said Edna thoughtfully.

"It must have been this morning after recess, when we went in," said Angel.

"It looks nice," said Rags again, tearfully.

"It does look kind of sweet," said one of the girls in the crowd, the same one who had said Rags had pretty brown eyes.

Rags was still sniffling when Miss Peters came out and asked what had happened. Angel told her. Then Miss Peters suggested that, since it was so late in the day, Angel could take Rags home and settle him down. "Maybe it wasn't a good idea for me to allow him to stay outside alone this morning," she said worriedly.

Angel wasn't sure, but she thought Miss Peters looked relieved as they turned to walk home.

Rags had stopped crying by now, and Angel didn't want him to get started all over again, so she decided not to remind him that they were going to take his name away and recement the walk. But she was worried about the money they owed the school and about Father Ryan's call on Monday.

When they got home they sat on the back steps. Angel let Bubba out in the yard, and he rolled in the dirt in the garden and then stood up and shook himself.

"Bubba's dirty," said Rags.

"Maybe we should give him a bath before Alyce comes home," said Angel. Angel was beginning to feel pressured by all the things a person in charge has to do. She felt angry at her mother for going away and angry at Alyce for going to the hospital. And she was sure of one thing. By the time her mother returned, she would need a vacation more than her mother ever had.

7

A VISIT TO THE HOSPITAL

Angel and Rags each ate one of Alyce's diet dinners for supper. When they were through, Angel said, "Maybe we should go to the hospital and see Alyce. We could take her some flowers or something."

"The hospital?" Rags looked interested.

"You visit people in hospitals," said Angel. "To make them feel better." Even as she said it, she knew it wasn't the real reason. Angel was dreading another night alone in the house, which she now felt sure was haunted. And she was becoming increasingly worried about Father Ryan's call on Monday. Maybe she could confess to Alyce — about the sidewalk, Margaret Toomer, everything.

Angel cleared the table and did the dishes. There were only two forks and two bowls. Then she watered Alyce's plants and fed the animals.

"We could take her some flowers and then come home and go to bed early." Angel felt as if she had not slept for weeks. It was hard to believe that it had been only last night that the strange noises had kept her up. So much had happened since then. She would give Rags his bath and some clean pajamas, take a nice warm bath herself, and then make up the sleep she had lost the night before. Angel made up her mind that she would not hear noises tonight, not ghosts or burglars or anything else. She was too tired to waste time being frightened.

Angel sent Rags out in the yard to pick the last of the autumn asters, which were just a little bit brown around the edges. "Pick everything you can find," she told him.

Rags came in with six asters, a daisy, a hollyhock, and two carrot tops. "Everything is dead," said Rags sadly.

"Those look fine," said Angel. She wrapped the stems in a wet paper towel as she'd seen her mother do, and they set off for the hospital, a few blocks away.

"Now don't get into any hospital trouble," said Angel, remembering the cement. As they walked in the front entrance, Rags wrinkled up his nose.

"What's that smell?" he said.

"Medicine," said Angel. "And maybe some germs mixed in."

The children walked down a long hallway that seemed endless. Angel began to wonder how they would ever find Alyce.

"Where's Alyce?" said Rags, looking into the rooms opening off the hallway.

"She's in one of these rooms. We just have to look, I suppose."

Rags and Angel looked into each room along the hallway. Some of the people were very friendly and invited them to come in and visit, but Rags said, "We have to find Alyce."

When they were halfway down the hall, a nurse who was pushing a cart full of flowers said, "What are you children doing here?"

"We have to find Alyce," said Rags.

"She's our babysitter," said Angel. "And our friend," she added. After all, Alyce was not a real babysitter. She was just a friend who happened to babysit.

"Children are not allowed in the hospital," said the nurse firmly. "You will have to leave," she insisted.

Before Rags could launch into his story about Alyce again, Angel said, "We'll go."

The nurse nodded and, picking up a vase of flowers, she went into one of the rooms.

"Whose flowers are those?" said Rags.

"They're for patients," said Angel. "Come on, Rags. We'll find Alyce and give her the flowers and then we'll leave."

"Is Alyce patient?"

"Alyce is *a* patient," said Angel, running ahead and checking the rooms quickly. She noticed after a few glances that the names were on the doors, which made the search much easier.

When she'd checked all the rooms in that hall, she summoned Rags and started down a hall that went in another direction. By the time Rags joined her, he was carrying three roses and some carnations along with the withered asters.

"Where did you get those?" a horrified Angel asked.

"For Alyce," said Rags. "From the cart."

"Those belong to the patients," said Angel, very impatiently.

"You said Alyce is a patient," retorted Rags. "You said so."

Angel reached for the flowers, intending to return them to the cart, but when she thought about explaining to the angry nurse what had happened, she decided against it.

"Rags, don't let any nurses see you. Let's find Alyce and get out of here."

As they crept quietly along the hall checking rooms, they heard babies crying. Angel followed the sound.

"Oh Rags! Look! Look at the tiny babies!" Inside a nursery, rows of tiny bassinets held babies wrapped in pink and blue blankets.

Rags looked through the glass window. "Are they sick? Are the babies sick?"

"Of course not," said Angel. "Oh look, Rags, that one is smiling!"

"Why are they in the hospital if they aren't sick?"

"This is where mothers get babies, Rags, in the hospital. You know that."

Rags was deep in thought. So much that was new had happened to him in the last few days. It was hard to take it all in.

"Are the mothers sick then, Angel?"

"No, Rags."

"Then why do they get them in the hospital?" he demanded. Rags looked as though he might cry.

"I don't know, they just do." Her mother had long ago discussed the facts of life with Angel, but she wasn't sure how to explain it all to Rags. Rags didn't look satisfied. "They have to get them somewhere, don't they? What's the difference where?"

"Did I come from this hospital?" he demanded.

"Yes," said Angel.

"Did you?"

"Yes."

"Did Alyce?"

"No. I don't know."

"Who put those babies here?"

Angel sighed. She wished her mother had done a better job telling Rags the facts of life. Now here she was again, because of her mother's shortcomings, having to pacify Rags and tell him things his own mother should have told him long ago. She might as well be Rags's mother!

"Who put those babies here?" demanded Rags again, more loudly.

"I suppose the doctor."

"Where'd he get them?"

"From the mothers."

"You said mothers got them at the hospital, Angel!" Now Rags looked really upset.

Someone in white was coming toward them. Angel grabbed Rags and pushed him ahead of her in the other direction.

"*Shsssh*," she said. "You know about seeds and stuff," she whispered. "Didn't Mom tell you?"

Rags shook his head.

"Well, babies come from seeds, I think, just like flowers."

114

Rags thought of the asters he'd picked in the back yard.

"Just believe me, Rags! Don't you dare ask me anything else. Babies come from seeds, and that's it." She anxiously checked the next few doors.

"Finally!" said Angel in relief. "Here is Alyce's room!"

Angel couldn't believe her eyes. They went into the room, and there was Alyce in bed, with one leg all encased in white plaster. Alyce was watching television and eating candy out of a white box and laughing out loud.

Rags ran up to her and said, "Babies come from seeds!"

"We brought you some flowers," said Angel, quickly changing the subject.

Alyce put both her arms out to welcome them, and said, "Why my little darlings! Come to see Alyce — all this way to see Alyce! Are you all right? Let me look at you!"

"We can't stay," said Angel. "Children aren't supposed to be here. The nurse told us."

Alyce waved her hand, as if to discard the unpleasant thought. "Maxine," she called to the woman in the next bed, "these are my little charges, Angel and Rags O'Leary!"

Maxine, who was knitting something long and pink and narrow, reached out to shake Angel's and Rags's hands and said she was glad to meet them. She had heard all about them, she said.

"Babies come from seeds," Rags said, shaking her hand.

"What are you here for?" said Angel very quickly and politely when she saw the bewildered look on Maxine's face.

"Female trouble," said Maxine.

"That's too bad," said Angel politely. Female meant women. What trouble did women have? Trouble cooking? Maybe she had burned herself.

"Alyce is broken," said Rags. "That's why she's here."

Rags made a sawing motion across the cast on Alyce's leg.

"What lovely flowers!" said Alyce. "Ask the nurse for a vase, Angel."

Not on your life, thought Angel. Who knew what that mean nurse would do if she saw them here still — and with stolen flowers from her cart.

"I'll put them in this glass right here," said Angel, filling it with water at the sink.

"How are Bubba and Clarence and Tootsie?" asked Alyce. "And Margaret?"

"Bubba's dirty," said Rags. "But Margaret . . ."

"Margaret is fine," said Angel, slipping her hand over Rags's mouth before he could launch into the whole story of what had happened. "They are all fine," said Angel.

Alyce pointed to two chairs, and Angel and Rags sat down while Alyce told them about everyone in all the rooms around her. "And Mrs. Markly got hit by a car on Main Street," she wound up cheerfully.

Then she told them what the doctor had said about her broken bones, and that she could mend just as well at home, so she would see them tomorrow. And not to worry — she would take a taxicab home to her little darlings and never have to leave them again. "And you be sure to tell Margaret as soon as you get home!" finished Alyce.

Angel tried hard to say, "Margaret isn't there!" and "I lied," but she couldn't. Instead she stood up and said goodbye, waving to Maxine on her way out. She took Rags's hand and pulled him out the door, too. The mean nurse was coming toward them, pushing a cart of test tubes and rubber hoses. Alyce was calling out orders to them as they ran down the hall and out a rear exit.

It wasn't easy to undo a lie, thought Angel. And the longer one waited, the more complicated it became, one lie piling atop another. Angel wondered if she would ever be able to trust herself again. But today was not the time to come clean.

Angel chattered all the way home to keep Rags's mind off any baby-seed questions. It was late when they arrived home, and she hurried him through his bath and into his pajamas. But just as he was about to climb into bed, he said, "Angel, how can babies come out of seeds?" Angel knew that instead of climbing into her warm bed she would have to do something about Rags's questions or she wouldn't have a moment's peace.

She got the children's encyclopedia that she remembered reading when she was small, with the colored pictures of the insides of men and women, and read it to Rags. She showed him the pictures, but when she was through Rags looked more confused than ever. He said, "But how do babies come out of seeds?"

Angel slammed the book shut. "That's

positively *all* I know about babies, Rags. You'll just have to ask Mom when she gets home."

8

MORE NOISES IN THE NIGHT

After Rags had fallen asleep, Angel wondered why she had been in such a hurry to discourage his baby questions. By the time she was ready for bed herself and saw how dark it was outside, she wished that she had offered to let him come into her own room to continue the discussion.

Surely it would be better with Rags sitting on the floor beside her asking his eternal baby-seed questions, even if it lasted all night long, than it was to be alone in the dark room with no one to talk to. The questions would have distracted her from thoughts of ghosts, at least. Well, it was too late now. She could hear Rags snoring lightly (their mother said it was just loud breathing), and it would be selfish to wake him up.

Angel got up and moved her umbrella closer to her bed. She had taken it out of the closet again tonight. Then she climbed into bed and told herself she had a wild imagination. Just when she almost believed it, she heard a *scratch, scratch, scratch*. It seemed very close to her right ear.

Angel sat up in bed and looked at the black tree branches outside her window, waving back and forth in the wind. They're rubbing the roof, thought Angel, that's what's making that scratching noise. She fell back onto her pillow and had just closed her eyes when the squeaking began again. Was it footsteps on the stairs? Was something coming up slowly, slowly, toward her room?

Why didn't Rags wake up? How could he

sleep through a ghost-ridden, burglar-ridden night again? How selfish of Rags, leaving her to cope with this crisis all alone! It would be up to her, as usual, to save them both.

Angel crept out of bed and tiptoed to her dresser to look for something heavy. The heaviest thing there was her silver piggy bank full of pennies. She put it next to the umbrella. Then she sat on the edge of her bed trying to decide what her next move should be.

Squeak, squeak, scratch, scratch. There it was again. It was definitely not coming from the roof. This noise was in the very room she was in. Angel was too terrified to move, too frightened to get up to turn on the light. She might bump into the intruder, head-on!

She drew her nightgown around her, and as she did, she felt something brush across her feet. Was it her nightgown? No, there it was again. Something was actually walking across her feet! Something sharp! She drew her feet up on the bed beside her and pulled the covers over her head. Now she felt something on her legs! Something was in bed with her! A small ghost with sharp feet or maybe even a vampire! Some bloodthirsty creature who had waited until the children were alone in the house and now had found its chance.

Angel threw off the covers and screamed. She screamed all the way to Rags's room, where she threw herself on his bed in terror.

Rags sighed in his sleep, turned over, and began his loud breathing again. He hadn't heard a sound. Angel began to shake him by the shoulders and shout into his ear.

"Rags! Get up, Rags! There is someone in this house!"

Rags sat up and listened, but as soon as Angel let go of his shoulders, he fell backward onto his pillow and was asleep again. Angel could not believe it. Why, the whole house could come down around him, and Rags would sleep on. Angel shook him again, and this time she pushed him out of his bed into a standing position.

"Rags!" she said clearly and loudly. "There is someone in this house!"

"Who?" said Rags.

"How would I know?" said Angel angrily. "A ghost or a burglar or a vampire!"

Rags was wide awake. He knew Angel wouldn't lie to him. "Call the police!" he screamed, embracing the disaster now wholeheartedly.

Angel considered calling, but just for a second or two. The police were getting to be almost like part of the family. The neighbors would tell her mother about how often they came with sirens and whistles and axes — it would be awful. As frightened as Angel was, she didn't want the police in the house again.

"We can handle it," said Angel, not believing her own words for one minute.

"We can handle it," repeated Rags,

throwing things out of his drawers in search of a weapon of his own. Finding only underwear, he turned to his closet and picked up a small red metal shovel, which he slung over his shoulder.

Angel's screams had awakened the animals, and they could hear Bubba now, howling in the living room. Clarence, although he had a cover over his cage, was singing lustily. As Angel started for her own room to arm herself, Tootsie shot down the hall, his white fur standing on end and his tail straight in the air. He was hissing. Maybe cats caught vampires, she thought. Maybe Tootsie would save them.

But as Angel picked up her umbrella and piggy bank, Tootsie dove under her bed and refused to come out. He's as scared as we are, thought Angel.

There was so much other noise in the house now that she could no longer hear the scratching and squeaking. Just as she and Rags got to the top of the stairs with their weapons, they heard something running through the house.

"Is that the vampire?" whispered Rags loudly.

"That's something bigger than a vampire!" whispered Angel, trembling all over. "That is something as big as a person!"

"A ghost!" said Rags, rolling his eyes.

"A ghost doesn't sound that — heavy," said Angel. "Ghosts are like air. They don't bump into furniture and make a lot of noise running."

The running got louder and louder. And Bubba's barking got louder and louder along with it.

Just when Angel thought that all this noise would surely bring the police unsummoned, there was an even louder noise below them — a series of crashes, beginning with a heavy metal sound and ending with a glassy tinkling noise, like something fragile breaking. Angel screamed again, and Tootsie shot past them down the hall, hair on end and back arched. He disappeared down the stairs into the dark living room below.

Rags clung to Angel, whimpering now and repeating, "I want Mom. I want Mom."

Suddenly, all the noises came to an abrupt stop — the running, the chasing, the barking, the singing. It was so quiet now that Angel could hear the trees whispering in the breeze outside. Even Rags was quiet.

"We have to go down there, Rags. We have to see what happened."

"I don't want to," whispered Rags, on the verge of tears. "I want Mom."

"Mom's gone, and we have to see what happened. Now be brave, Rags. I can't go down alone. I *need* you."

Rags wiped his eyes and stood up straight. If Angel needed him, he would have to try to be brave.

With a firm grip on their weapons, they started down the stairs on their tiptoes. When they got to the bottom, Angel turned on the overhead light in the living room and bathed the room in light. Angel and Rags stared at the disaster all around them. Chairs were overturned, books and magazines were in disarray, vases had spilled, and pictures on the wall were askew. An end table was on its side, and the lamp that had been on it was on the floor, broken into pieces. Shattered glass was everywhere.

"Is there a body?" whispered Rags.

Angel had been thinking the same thing. On television when a lamp was broken, there was usually a body on the floor beside it. Detectives came then and roped the area off and told the family not to touch a thing until they took fingerprints.

"Of course not!" said Angel in disgust. "Whose body would it be?"

"The body of the ghost," whispered Rags. "Or a burglar."

"There's no body," said Angel firmly, after checking carefully to make sure.

When the children walked further into the room, they saw something else. Bubba was

sniffing the overturned furniture. He seemed excited and was breathing heavily.

And on the floor, washing his face, was Tootsie.

"Look!" shouted Rags. "Something's on the floor in front of Tootsie!" He pointed.

Angel walked closer to Tootsie and put her foot on something brown in front of her.

"It's a mouse!" she shrieked. "It's a — dead mouse! Myron's mouse! Rags, that's our ghost. Our burglar. Our vampire."

The children sat down on the couch. Angel felt like a detective.

"Do you know what I think?" she said.

Rags shook his head.

"I think," she went on, "that Myron's mouse made the scratching and squeaking noises I heard. And I think he was in my bedroom and walked over my feet!"

"Who was running?" said Rags. "Who knocked all this stuff over?" Rags waved his arm at the damage.

"Bubba," said Angel. Bubba stopped his

sniffing at the sound of his name and came and laid his head on Angel's lap.

"I think when I screamed, the mouse ran downstairs and Bubba woke up and started barking and chasing it. Then when Tootsie came downstairs he caught it! Tootsie caught the burglar!"

"Good kitty," said Rags, petting Tootsie and getting his pajamas covered with white cat hair.

Tootsie threw the dead mouse into the air and tried to catch it.

"Poor mousie," said Rags.

"Myron will have to get a new pet," said Angel. "We have to clean this up," she added, looking around the room.

The children got the broom and dustpan and swept and cleaned and set the over-turned furniture upright. Rags took the dead mouse from Tootsie and put it in a small Kleenex box for future burial. By the time they were through cleaning up, it was one o'clock in the morning.

"It looks like nothing ever happened," said Angel wearily, throwing herself onto the couch.

"Except the lamp," said Rags. "The lamp is gone."

"Maybe Mom won't notice," said Angel. "No one ever uses that lamp." Just one more thing to hide, thought Angel. One more secret that would need to be guarded.

Angel and Rags climbed the stairs together. Rags put his shovel away, and Angel returned the umbrella to her closet and the bank to its place on her dresser. She threw herself into her peaceful bed, which only hours before had been a place of terror. In a few minutes she was asleep, and she didn't see the sky getting light in the east.

9

ANGEL TELLS ALL

Angel and Rags slept late on Saturday morning. When Angel looked at her little clock it said eleven o'clock. She walked into Rags's room and found him still asleep. Half an hour later, she began to wonder if Rags would ever wake up on his own at all. Perhaps he'd sleep straight through the day until the next night! It seemed to Angel that when her mother was home, Rags was the first one up, climbing into bed with one of them and bouncing about until they got up, too. Things were certainly different without her. She thought about how much she missed her mother and felt like crying. But she felt angry, too, and resolved not to speak to her when she did return.

"Rags," called Angel finally. "It's time to get up." She picked Rags's clothes up from the floor and put them into the clothes hamper. It was full. The towels from Rags's bath the night before didn't even fit into the hamper.

We have to wash clothes, thought Angel, wondering if she dared operate the washing machine on her own.

By the time the children were through with breakfast, Alyce had arrived at the door, home from the hospital in a taxicab.

"Alyce!" shouted Rags, throwing his arms around her, crutches and all. Alyce stood at the door with tears in her eyes. At first Angel thought she was in pain, but then she saw that she was crying because she was so glad to be back. Angel felt she was being overly dramatic, but it was good to see her anyway, even if it was more work when she was here than when they were alone. Now, Angel thought, it would be even more work since Alyce was on crutches.

"I just couldn't wait to get here," said Alyce. "I left early, even though I had my dinner coming for the day. It was beef stroganoff with fresh asparagus." She seemed to savor the thought.

Alyce hobbled into the dining room, bringing a whiff of hospital smell with her. Her cast was large and white and took up a lot of space in a room. She set her crutches against the wall and limped to a chair, falling heavily into it.

"I'm so glad to be home," said Alyce again, smiling. She looked around at the house as if she was expecting something new and different. Tootsie rubbed against her legs, and Bubba was wagging his tail. "Where is Margaret?" asked Alyce.

"Gone," said Angel quickly. "She had to go to see her daughter in Madison. She knew you were coming today." Alyce looked satisfied.

"We found Myron's pet," said Rags, "but we . . ."

Here Angel interrupted him. There was no need to tell Alyce about last night's chase in detail — or the sidewalk — or the broken lamp. No use looking for trouble. There was enough trouble without bringing up things that were over and past.

"Now," said Alyce. "Tell me everything. What did you two do while I was gone?"

Angel shot a warning glance at Rags.

He looked like he was bursting at the seams, but he sat quietly, waiting for a cue from Angel.

"Nothing much," said Angel. "Nothing much at all. We ate the diet dinners and watered your plants and fed the animals and played with Edna and went to school and went to bed every night. Same as always," she added.

Angel wondered when Alyce would see

Margaret and what would happen when she discovered the truth.

She hoped Alyce would stay away from the subject and that it would never come up again.

"Maybe you should lie down," said Angel kindly.

"No, no, I am going to try to be up and around," said Alyce. "I'm no invalid, you know."

"Do you want some lunch?" asked Angel, wondering what there was left to eat in the house.

"Later on," said Alyce. "Dear me, we must be all out of food." She frowned.

Angel nodded. "And we're all out of clean clothes and towels," she said.

"Well, we can wash clothes, can't we?" said Alyce brightly.

Angel was sure that the *we* was *I*, herself. Angel. Alyce couldn't get down to the basement on those crutches.

"I'll get the clothes," said Angel.

She and Alyce sorted the clothes into different piles, and Alyce explained to Angel which knobs to turn and which dials to set.

"Put just one-half cup of soap in," Alyce called down the steps.

Angel turned the dials and knobs she'd been told to turn and then went upstairs to make her bed while Alyce hobbled around the house looking things over and describing her hospital experiences.

Later, Angel and Rags wrote their names on Alyce's cast, and Rags drew a little picture of a police car. After lunch, Alyce insisted that it would be no trouble at all for her to do the dishes — she could stand on one leg just fine. "No sense in babying myself," she said.

Angel went out and sat on the back steps. Although Alyce was home and things were almost normal, she had a nagging feeling that would not go away. She had to do something about those lies. They would keep piling up otherwise, and pretty soon she wouldn't know what was true and what was made up. She had intended to wait for the right time, but there probably was no right time, she now had to admit to herself reluctantly. The right time is right this minute, she decided.

Angel got up and walked into the house. Alyce had finished the dishes without injuring herself and was looking over her hospital bills at the dining room table. "One dollar, Angel! Just for one little pain pill! It's good I came home when I did."

Angel nodded. She sat down on a chair at the table, planning to say in her most grown-up manner, "May I talk to you about something?" But instead she heard her voice shouting, "I lied! Margaret Toomer is in Madison. She didn't stay with us!"

Alyce looked up from her bills in surprise. Angel waited for her to scold, to tell her how irresponsible she was in an emergency. Instead Alyce sat quietly for a moment. Then she got up and hobbled over to Angel and put her arm around her.

"That must have been very hard for you to tell me," she said.

"It was," said Angel, now in tears.

"It was very brave of you to take charge," said Alyce. "I don't know many children who would do that."

Angel sniffed. She couldn't believe her ears.

"You did it to spare me worry," Alyce went on. "Weren't you frightened, in the house alone all night?"

"Yes," said Angel, wiping her eyes. She went on to tell Alyce all about the two nights and Myron's mouse and the broken lamp, and as she told it, she realized that here in the broad daylight it didn't feel scary at all.

"My poor dears!" said Alyce, hugging Angel closer and hugging Rags as well when he wandered in.

Since her confession had gone so well,

Angel decided to press on with the sidewalk story and get everything out into the open, once and for all. She told Alyce the whole story and then said, "There!"

Alyce took a bit longer this time to react. Finally she said, "Is there anything else, Angel? Is there anything else that I don't know?"

"I think that's all," said Angel.

Alyce breathed a sigh of relief. "Good," she said. "Well, Rags didn't know any better, poor dear," she cooed. "And you did what you felt you had to do, taking him to school. After all, you couldn't have left him alone. No, it's not your fault either. Live and learn, I say. We will always remember this, won't we, Angel? And if anything like this should happen again, you'll ask an adult for help, won't you?"

Angel nodded. She certainly would.

"There is," Alyce went on, "the sidewalk to consider." She frowned.

"We have to pay," said Angel.

Alyce thought some more. "Let me think about it for a while," she said.

Angel felt a surge of warmth for Alyce because she was being so understanding, but she also felt a bit cross with her for taking it so well. It didn't seem right that they weren't being chastised in some way. Angel liked a person who took things in hand, who kept order and sanity and could be counted on to be angry when things went wrong — like her mother. Alyce went to lie down while Angel hung the clothes to dry. Then Angel took Rags outside to play.

At dinner that night Alyce said, "You know, someone has to pay for the sidewalk. It doesn't seem fair for your mother to pay, does it?"

"Rags and I will pay for it," said Angel, "but we aren't sure how to earn money."

"I think," said Alyce, "that you should tell your mother the story, and perhaps she will have some jobs for you to do to work the bill off. You know, extra things this fall. She'll probably be busier than ever at work when she returns from her vacation and will need a great deal of help at home."

Angel had underestimated Alyce again. She was really very wise. That was a good idea. And it was a relief telling the whole truth, as she had come to discover.

"That's a good idea," said Angel. "Thank you, Alyce. That's just what we'll do."

"After she's been home a while . . ." added Alyce. "I mean, one shouldn't bring up anything disturbing the minute someone comes home from a pleasant trip."

Angel knew what Alyce meant. She would definitely let her mother come home to peaceful surroundings. There would be plenty of time to tell her before the bill from the principal came in the mail.

The next few days passed quite routinely. Alyce talked to Father Ryan, and Angel went to school and came home and did her homework. Not a single emergency occurred. The following week Alyce got a walking cast and could move around very well.

And then one day Angel walked in the back door after school and saw suitcases piled up on the floor. She smelled her mother's talcum powder, and best of all, she heard her mother's voice coming from the living room.

Angel flew into the living room, and there she was! Sitting on the couch holding Rags — in her own home where she belonged. The whole room looked much brighter with her mother in it. Just seeing her again made Angel realize that she could not hold a grudge. She forgave her mother on sight for going away.

"Angel!" Mrs. O'Leary had tears in her eyes, but her face looked bright and fresh and alive. With a start Angel saw her as if for the first time — a real person with a life of her own — someone who could do exciting things and have fun. Her mother looked younger than Angel remembered. Too

young to be Angel's mother. Too young to deal with police cars and runaway mice and cement-writing children. Her mother could probably exist very well without her children.

Mrs. O'Leary stood up and put out her arms and Angel ran toward her, crying and hugging her at the same time. "I thought you'd never come home," said Angel.

"I'm so glad to be home!" said Mrs. O'Leary at the same time.

"Are you really?" said Angel in surprise.

"Awfully glad. All I could think of was you and Rags. That's why we came home early."

For someone who had been thinking only of her children, her mother appeared to have had a very good time, Angel thought later as she was listening to her mother's stories about Canada and the handsome Frenchman she had met and how she and Beth had gotten lost in Toronto and about the French restaurant in Winnipeg. Then Mrs. O'Leary opened a suitcase and gave Angel a small box with a tiny gold locket and a matching narrow gold bracelet in it. Angel put them on and cried all over again, she was so happy. Mrs. O'Leary had presents for Alyce and Rags, too, and her face glowed, watching them open the packages.

"I think this trip was a very, very good thing for all of you," said Alyce wisely. "You'll be seeing each other with brand new eyes for a while."

Angel looked at Alyce. Her hair looked grayer than when she had come, and she looked — older, somehow. It wasn't easy minding children, Angel knew, thinking of Rags. She went over and gave Alyce a small hug. She could afford to do that now that her visit had come to an end. Why, she might even miss her.

"And Angel was in charge!" her mother was saying. "Imagine Alyce in the hospital, and my not knowing! I would have caught a plane right home, had I known."

"And your trip would have been ruined," said Angel. "We got along just fine. We really did." At that moment Angel really believed it. She didn't remember having any problems.

"Well, all's well that ends well, they say," said Alyce cheerfully.

"I'm glad you had a wonderful trip," said Angel. "Will this vacation last you a few years?" she asked, looking anxious.

"More than a few years," her mother said, and laughed.

It was good to hear her laugh again.

As Alyce began to relate some of her hospital experiences and Rags showed his mother his drawing and writing papers, Edna came to the back door. Angel went out on the back steps and sat with her. Edna looked upset.

"What's the matter, Edna?" said Angel, in alarm.

A tear rolled down Edna's cheek. "My mom is going out of town!" she said. "My dad is taking a business trip, and my mom is going along!" She put her chin in her hands and looked sad.

"But you wanted your mom to go away!" said Angel. "You said you like to be in charge!"

Edna didn't say anything. She just sat there, her shoulders slumping down, looking dejected. Angel put her arm around her. Edna had always seemed so sure of herself. Angel felt surprised, but rather good also, that Edna wasn't strong all the time. She had moments, just like Angel, when she was scared.

Angel told her that the time would go fast and before she knew it her mother would be back again. Then she showed her the bracelet and locket, and suddenly Angel was the one who was loved and cared for and Edna had become the orphan. Life held all kinds of surprises, thought Angel.

Before dinner Alyce went home, and the house looked bare without all of her things.

It was quiet with no barking and singing from Bubba and Clarence. Angel's mother seemed to put her touch on everything as she passed it, and soon it felt as if she had never been away, except for the spring in her step and the way she kept looking so young.

That night they had a lovely dinner together by candlelight, with real food. Angel, Rags, and their mother.

After dinner Mrs. O'Leary told them more stories about Canada, and finally they went upstairs together to get ready for bed.

As Angel crawled into her bed with no mouse or burglar worries, the last thing she heard before falling asleep was Rags asking her mother, "How do babies come out of seeds?"

Angel snuggled deeper under the covers. She thought she heard her mother saying (or did she dream it?) "Let's get the children's encyclopedia out . . ."

Angel smiled in her dream, knowing that Rags would not be put off with the encyclopedia for long. But it was her mother's problem now, not hers.